Snowball Express

Books by Joe Claro
available from Scholastic

Meatballs

Snowball Express

from the Walt Disney Productions film

Snowball Express

book by

Joe Claro

screenplay by

Don Tait and
Jim Parker &
Arnold Margolin

directed by

Norman Tokar

based on the book, Chateau Bon Vivant, by

Frankie and John O'Rear

SCHOLASTIC BOOK SERVICES

NEW YORK • TORONTO • LONDON • AUCKLAND • SYDNEY • TOKYO

To
Chris, Danielle, Noel,
Nicole, and Natasha

ISBN 0-590-30359-7

 This edition is published by Scholastic Book Services, a division of Scholastic Magazines, Inc., by arrangement with Walt Disney Productions, Inc.

12 11 10 9 8 7 6 5 4 3 2 1 2 0 1 2 3 4 5/8

Printed in the U.S.A. 06

Snowball Express

The early morning stillness in the Baxter apartment was broken by a low woof. Strongheart, the family's St. Bernard, was greeting the dawn — and also discreetly reminding his slug-a-bed family that it was time to *eat*.

It wasn't six a.m. yet. But Strongheart was on the alert when Mrs. Sue Baxter came sleepily out of the bedroom.

"Hi, boy," she said softly. "Just a second."

She disappeared into the kitchen. Strongheart was pleased to hear the refrigerator door open and slam shut, and even more pleased to hear the clatter of his bowl on the kitchen floor.

He leaned against the gate that kept him in the entrance hall. He could easily have knocked it down. But he was too polite to do that.

In a few seconds, Sue invited him into the kitchen. A few seconds after that, he had gulped down his morning meal and helped himself to a refreshing swig of water. Then he flopped across the small kitchen floor.

"Out, boy!" Sue said firmly. "Out! In a kitchen this size, you could pass for wall-to-wall carpeting. Go check the rest of the family."

Strongheart gave her a glance, lumbered to his feet, and thumped out. He eased on down the hallway. Just as he reached his master's bedroom, he heard the usual six o'clock alarm buzz. He peered into Johnny and Sue's bedroom.

Johnny Baxter was reaching for the alarm button. "I've never seen an alarm clock I couldn't learn to hate," he grumbled. He turned the alarm off and punched his face into his pillow.

Strongheart padded into the room. He heaved his body onto the bed and snuggled close to his master. Still more than half asleep, Johnny reached up and patted Strongheart on the head.

"I know, dear," he said. "I'll be right up."

A kind greeting from his master was a rare thing. In gratitude, Strongheart raised his great head and turned it to plant a slobbery kiss all over an exposed ear.

Richard Baxter, aged twelve, stepped from

his bedroom just in time to hear his father roar, "Out! I said OUT!"

Richard rushed across the hallway. "Dad!" he said. "Don't shout at him! The vet said he's sensitive."

"Sensitive?" Johnny said, wrestling Strongheart from the bed. "For $26, a vet tells you he's sensitive? I tell you, Richard, that rug has got to go!"

Richard rushed in and threw his arms around Strongheart's neck. "Don't forget," he said sternly, "*I'm* sensitive too. He goes, I go."

"Well, right now," his father bellowed, "*I* go! To the bathroom. This ear has to be washed. *It's* sensitive! Out of my way, both of you!"

Johnny strode to the bathroom door, twisted the knob, and pushed. It was locked. "Oh no!" he groaned.

"Chris," Sue called from the kitchen which was within easy hearing of the bedroom area. "Chris! Don't tie up the bathroom, dear."

"Now you see what's happened?" Johnny groaned. "Your sister got there first."

Richard also groaned. "And we both know what that means! The day she turned 16, she set up camp in there!"

Not surprisingly, Chris was first to arrive

at the kitchen counter. "Morning, Mom," she said, lifting herself onto a stool. She dropped two slices of bread into the toaster in the same movement.

"Well, you look ready for the day," Sue said smiling.

"My turn to walk Strongheart," Chris sighed. "It's humiliating! Sometimes I think Dad is right. Strongheart should go back where he came from. The Alps, or wherever it is."

"It would break your brother's heart," Sue said.

"I never said Strongheart should go alone," Chris said. "Oh, you know, I had the weirdest dream last night. There was this sort of Tinkerbell-type character flying around the living room. And we were all going to make a wish. You were supposed to go first."

"And did I?" her mother asked with interest.

Chris shook her head. "I'll never know. My alarm rang. Hey, Mom, what would you have wished for? I mean, if the alarm hadn't rung?"

"Four bathrooms," Sue said promptly.

Johnny walked into the kitchen. "What's this about four bathrooms?"

"Just talk, dear," Sue said. "Here, have

some orange juice. Chris, butter the toast, will you?"

Johnny took the glass of juice. Chris got to work on several slices of toast.

"Dad," she said, "I was just telling Mom about a dream I had. We were each going to have one wish come true. What would you wish for?"

"Hot black coffee and lightly buttered toast."

"Hopeless parents," Chris said. "Wasting wishes like that. I know what *I'd* wish would happen. I mean, if we're only making silly wishes."

"What's that?" Johnny asked.

"That we could afford a dog-walker."

"Or afford a dog," her father said through a mouthful of toast. "If we had all the money I've spent on food for that mutt—"

He paused, trying to think of some clever way to end the sentence.

"We'd have a lot of money," he finished.

Strongheart ambled to the kitchen doorway.

"Don't worry, Strongheart," Sue said. "Daddy really loves you."

"Sue!" Johnny yelled. "Cut out the 'daddy' stuff, will you? I am *not* his daddy!"

Sue turned to Strongheart again. "Mr. Baxter really loves you," she said.

"How did I ever get mixed up with this bunch of wise guys?" Johnny said. "If I can have my coffee, I'll leave for the office. I'm *expected* there."

"But here, you're *loved*," Chris said, kissing her father's ear. "Right, Mom?"

"Right," Sue said. She kissed his other ear.

"National Ear Day," Johnny said, trying not to look too pleased. "Why do I have so much trouble keeping track of holidays?"

On the way to the office, it occurred to Johnny that nobody else seemed to be celebrating National Ear Day. The sounds of the subway and the traffic jam seemed designed to destroy as many ears as possible.

The friendly neighborhood jackhammer outside his office building was the last straw. By the time he reached the elevator, he was dreaming about living in a quiet cave.

Johnny had rushed, in a desperate effort to get to his office by nine o'clock. Once or twice a week, he failed to make it. This was one of those days. It was 9:01 when he walked in.

As usual, Mr. Carruthers was waiting for him. Mr. Carruthers was dependable. He could be relied on to make the same crack to every employee who came in after the stroke of nine.

"Good morning," Mr. Carruthers said with a sickly smile. "Nice of you to join us. We start at nine, you know."

Johnny winced. The best thing that could be said about Carruthers' routine was that it was over quickly. But this time, he added something new.

"Another thing, Baxter," he said. "We would appreciate it if you'd take care of your personal affairs on your own time."

He made a slight motion toward Johnny's desk. Johnny looked over and saw a stranger sitting there.

Carruthers added, "You might tell your Mr. Fowler that we have rules around here."

"Mr. Fowler?" Johnny asked. "Who's Mr. Fowler?"

"I suggest *you* find that out," Carruthers said. "Then you can explain our office policy to him."

For one glorious moment, Johnny considered calling the local bakery, buying a large cream pie, and tossing it at Mr. Carruthers' baggy face. Then a vision of Sue and the children rose before him. The moment passed, and Johnny marched to his desk.

Mr. Fowler stood up, briefcase in hand. "Mr. Baxter?" he asked.

Johnny nodded.

"John Sylvester Baxter?"

"Yes?"

"My name is Fowler. I'm from the law firm of Voorhees, Bruckner, and Voorhees."

Johnny turned pale. "A lawyer? Am I being sued?"

"Oh, nothing like that. But I'm afraid I have bad news for you."

Johnny turned a little paler. "What — kind — of — bad — news?" he asked.

"Jacob Barnsworth is dead," Mr. Fowler said sadly.

Johnny tried to share the sadness. Instead, he looked puzzled. "That's too bad," he said.

Johnny's puzzled look threw Mr. Fowler off. "You *are* John Sylvester Baxter, aren't you?"

"Yes, yes," Johnny said quickly. He was glad to hear a name he recognized.

"And your mother's maiden name was Pelton?"

"Yes. Judith Pelton. Judith Nash Pelton."

"So I thought," Mr. Fowler said, brightening. "Jacob *Nash* Barnsworth was your great-uncle. On your mother's side."

Johnny paused, thought hard, and suddenly smiled. "Yes!" he said. "Uncle Jake! My mother used to talk about him. Great guy. I guess. Too bad about Uncle Jake. I mean, too bad he died."

Mr. Fowler cleared his throat. "As far as we can determine, you are his next of kin and sole heir to his estate."

"Estate?" Johnny said in a solemn whisper.

Mr. Fowler slowly took some papers from his briefcase and looked through them. "Ah, yes," he said. "Here it is. The principal asset is the Grand Imperial Hotel. This property is in Silver Hill, Colorado. It's a small place, just 25 rooms. But it must be a fine investment. This letter states that the hotel was taking in over $14,000 a month."

Johnny stared with his mouth open.

"If you want," Mr. Fowler went on, "our office will take care of the transfer of title and the other arrangements. Mr. Baxter?"

Johnny continued to stare. Mr. Fowler had no way of knowing that John Sylvester Baxter was having a vision. It had to do with an enormous cream pie.

"Mr. Baxter?" Fowler repeated.

"Yes. Fine," Johnny said. "I'd appreciate that. Now, let me get this straight. I now *own* the Grand Imperial Hotel. In Silver Hill, Colorado. Is that right?"

"Lock, stock, and snowdrift," Mr. Fowler said, chuckling. "And, oh, yes, here's a letter from a Mr. Ridgeway of Silver Hill. He might be interested in the property if you decide to sell." He handed the letter to Johnny.

"Sell?" Johnny said blankly. "Oh, no, thank you. I don't think I'll—you *did* say $14,000 a month, didn't you?"

"Yes," the lawyer said. "Well, I'll be on my way. Here is my business card, if you wish to call us about anything."

Mr. Fowler was hardly out the door when a new John Sylvester Baxter leaped to his feet. He loudly announced his resignation to his co-workers. He made quite a speech, cheered on by a roomful of well-wishers. The noise brought Mr. Carruthers, who came striding in to restore order.

"Baxter," he said icily, "may I ask what you think you're doing?"

Johnny grinned. "I'm giving my farewell address to the troops."

"You're *leaving* the company?"

"Right this minute."

It wasn't until he was on the elevator that Johnny remembered Chris's dream. "I got my *real* wish!" he said out loud. "I'm leaving that job! Wait till I tell them! I can just see the looks on their faces!"

He decided to take a walk in the park and hold his surprise until after dinner.

*   *

He had expected them to be surprised. But *stunned*, *horrified*, and *furious* were the words he heard tossed around after his announcement.

"You just *quit*?" Chris asked. "Just like that? You actually quit your job?"

"Did I ever," Johnny said, grinning. "I may never forget the look on Carruthers' face. I'm through with Indemnity and Casualty forever. It's a new life for us. In Silver Hill, Colorado!"

Chris rushed from the room; they all heard the slam of her bedroom door.

Richard looked as though he'd just been chased through a cemetery by an unseen attacker. "Silver Hill, Colorado! Where's — "

"Richard," Sue said, "I think you'd better go to your room. Your father and I have some things to discuss."

"Yeah," muttered Richard. "I can see that."

"Johnny," Sue said when they were gone, "you've invested 11 years with that company. How can you throw it away? What about your dream of being office manager?"

"Well," he said, "I suddenly realized that I don't *want* to be an office manager. In 11 years, all I've ever done is move from accounts receivable to accounts payable. I've been digging myself into a hole in that job. Today, somebody threw me a rope."

"So you're going to toss everything away and drag your family into the wilderness."

"What wilderness, Sue? I'm taking over as owner of the Grand Imperial Hotel! Twenty-five rooms! Fourteen thousand a month! Does that sound like wilderness to you?"

"You've chucked away our lives on the word of some stranger."

"Sue," Johnny said, standing over her, "this is the kind of chance most people never get. A chance to stand on your own two feet, to get out of this smogpot and go where the sky is blue."

Sue stood up and stormed out of the room, slamming the door behind her. Strongheart yawned, shook himself, and padded off into the kitchen.

Alone, Johnny clenched his fists and yelled at the closed door. "Run out if you want to! But this family is moving to Silver Hill!" No response. "Colorado!"

It took the Baxters five days to drive to the Colorado state line. That was two days longer than it had taken Johnny to arrange things for the move.

The landlord had given him no trouble at all about breaking his lease. In New York City, a three-bedroom apartment is as rare as a smile in a dentist's waiting room. And with a new tenant, the landlord could automatically raise the rent.

Johnny had arranged with a neighbor to see that the movers took everything. He'd had Chris's and Richard's school records transferred, paid his garage bill, and left his forwarding address with the post office.

During all this, he'd paid as little attention as possible to the constant grumbling around him. He *knew* this was the chance of a lifetime. His wife and children were too concerned with such trivial things as friends, relatives, and familiar surroundings. They'd soon see how right he was.

Johnny had hoped to make the drive to Colorado in three days, but he was surrounded by hostile passengers. At the end of six or seven hours of riding each day, the complaints would begin. Before long, Johnny would be forced to stop for the night. He spent most of each night thinking of how many more miles they could have covered.

It was the early afternoon of the eighth day following Mr. Fowler's visit. They crossed the Colorado state line, and Johnny let out a whoop. It was the only whoop to be heard for miles around.

By this time, Johnny had grown used to being the only enthusiastic member of the family. The sulking would pass, he was sure. Just let them get a taste of what it meant to live where the air was free, the grass was green, and 25 rooms brought in $14,000 a month!

It was nearly time for dinner when the family passed a sign that said, "Silver Hill—10 miles."

"We've made it!" Johnny shouted. He pressed down on the gas pedal and belted out a one-man chorus of "She'll Be Comin' Round the Mountain." Not even Strongheart joined him in song.

The battered old station wagon bumped its way into the tiny town. A few passersby stared curiously at the overloaded car, piled high with suitcases, cardboard boxes, and two bicycles. On the back seat, Chris and Richard each hugged a window, staring glumly out. The window at the rear was open just enough for Strongheart to stick out his mighty head. Every now and then, he let out a gentle woof to let Silver Hill know that the Baxters had arrived.

The snow had been shoveled from Main Street, but the rest of the world was all one solid, white monotone.

Main Street itself was only three blocks long. The side streets were little more than alleys piled high with snow.

As the Baxters slowly drove past the small, rundown wooden buildings, Chris and Richard sank even lower on the back seats. Sue just stared, unable to believe they'd left everything behind for this place.

Johnny's singing turned to a thoughtful hum as he looked from side to side for the Grand Imperial Hotel.

They reached the end of the third block. It

was also the end of Main Street, and Johnny stopped the car.

"We seem to have missed the hotel," Sue said.

"Maybe we're in the wrong part of town," Richard added.

Johnny shook his head, a puzzled look on his face. "There's only one part," he said. "And we just saw it."

"Do you suppose Silver Hill has a suburb?" Chris asked. "Silver Hill Gardens, maybe? Silver Hill Estates?"

After five days of similar comments, Johnny had grown immune to sarcasm. He ignored his daughter and looked out his window. How could they have missed the Grand Imperial Hotel?

"There's a gas station up ahead," Sue said. "We'd better ask someone."

"Right," Johnny said, relieved to hear that there was something he could do. He drove into the gas station and honked his horn.

A young man came out, wiping his hands on a rag. He grinned when he saw the freight on top of the roof, took a long look at the license plate, and walked over to Johnny's window.

"You folks are from New York," he announced.

"That's right," Johnny said.

"Could tell by your license plate. We don't get many tourists here. Pretty far from the main road."

"We're not tourists," Johnny said. The young man checked the other passengers in the car. It was the first time he'd ever seen New Yorkers in real life.

"We're looking for the Grand Imperial Hotel," Johnny said.

But the young man wasn't listening. He had found a New Yorker who looked very interesting, indeed. He stared at Chris and wondered why she was frowning at him.

"Can you tell us how to get to it?" Johnny asked.

"Huh?"

"The Grand Imperial Hotel. My name's Baxter. I'm the new owner."

"Pleased to meet you, Mr. Baxter. I'm Wally. What did you say you were looking for?"

"The Grand Imperial Hotel," Johnny said, beginning to feel really annoyed.

"Never heard of it."

"This *is* Silver Hill, isn't it?"

"Yep."

"And you don't know the Grand Imperial Hotel?"

"Afraid not. And I've lived here all my life." Wally heard the girl in the back seat groan. He bent down and peered in. "Was it something I said?" he asked pleasantly.

Four or five of the passersby from Main Street had found their way to the gas station. They all stood around marveling at the foreign license plate and the condition of the car it was attached to.

An older man came out of the garage. "What's going on?" he asked Wally.

Turning to Johnny, Wally said, "This is my boss, Double L. Dingman. Mr. Dingman, meet Mr. Baxter."

Johnny smiled at Double L. Double L nodded.

"What's going on?" he repeated.

"These folks are from New York," Wally said. "They're looking for the Grand something-or-other."

"The Grand Imperial Hotel," Johnny said. Double L gave him a blank look. "It's supposed to be in Silver Hill."

Double L shrugged. "There's a Silver Hill in Wyoming," he said.

"No," Johnny said, his voice rising with each sentence. "Silver Hill, Colorado. The hotel belonged to the late Jacob Barnsworth."

"Jacob Barnsworth?" Double L said. "Jacob

— you mean old Crazy Jake?"

There was another groan. Wally was relieved to hear that this one came from the older woman in the front seat.

"Crazy Jake is dead," Wally said.

"I know that!" Johnny replied.

"You looking for Crazy Jake's place?" Double L asked. "It's about a mile further out."

"Right on this same road?" Johnny asked.

"No," Double L said. "Stay on this road till you pass Howard Babcock's place."

"Is there a sign or something?"

"The sign blew off," Wally said.

"You'll see three or four Holsteins near a red barn," Double L said.

"Holsteins?"

"Cows," Wally said helpfully. "They're from New York, Double L."

"Yeah, cows," Double L said. "Turn left at the little road just past the barn. That'll take you smack into the hotel. The Grand — what did you call it?"

Two voices from the back seat sang out, "The Grand Imperial Hotel!"

"Thanks," Johnny said, backing quickly out to the road.

"You folks related to Crazy Jake?" Double L called after them. Johnny pretended he didn't hear. He swung onto the road and down toward Howard Babcock's place.

After a few moments of silence, Richard asked, "*Are* you related to Crazy Jake, Dad?"

Johnny chose not to answer. "Keep your eyes open, everybody," Sue said. "We're looking for a red barn."

"With three or four Holsteins near it," Chris said. "Let's not forget the Holsteins."

The farther they drove from the gas station, the more dismal did the atmosphere in the car become. Even Johnny's pleasant face began to look grim.

As they passed the red barn, Richard rolled down his window. "Hi, Holsteins!" he called out.

"We'll have to remember to ask the Holsteins to dinner," Chris said. Strongheart woofed a greeting out the rear window.

They turned onto the little road Double L had described. The snow here hadn't been plowed, but some passing cars had made double tracks.

Johnny drove slowly to keep from skidding in the icy ruts. He slowed down even more as the road began to curve. At the end of the curve, he stopped.

There before them was the Grand Imperial Hotel.

"A dump by any other name," Sue said quietly, "would be the Grand Imperial Hotel."

No one else could speak. Four car doors opened. Four people and a large dog climbed out.

The large dog pranced around, glad to be free after so many hours. The four people stared open-mouthed at the building before them.

It was a two-story wooden frame building that might have been painted at the beginning of World War I. Then again, maybe not. Shingles and shutters hung loose at crazy angles. The front door was unlatched and creaked back and forth in the wind. One of the four steps leading up to the porch looked almost strong enough to support the weight of a six-year-old. The rest were either missing or in pieces.

Johnny cleared his throat. "Dad?" Richard said softly.

"Hm?" Johnny said, not taking his eyes off the building.

"How bad did you break things off with Mr. Carruthers?"

Johnny looked blankly at his son. Sue put her hand on Johnny's arm.

"Let's look inside," she said.

They stepped carefully onto the porch. Johnny held onto the door and wiped the snow away from its center window. There it was, etched in glass:

THE GRAND IMPERIAL HOTEL
FINEST IN LUXURY

They stepped into the lobby and found what must have once been a beautiful room. Fancy columns, real wooden paneling, three large fireplaces. If it hadn't been for the dust, the cobwebs, and a hint of ghosts in the icy gloom, this place could have been worth the trip.

"Brrr! It's even colder in here than outside," Chris said shivering.

Johnny snapped a light switch, but nothing happened.

"First thing tomorrow," he said, "we'll get the electricity back on." His voice was light, as he tried to lift the family mood. "Things will look better when we get a fire going. Richard, see if you can find something to burn."

"How about these chairs?" his son asked.

"Firewood," Johnny said. "Look over there in the wood box."

"Shouldn't we find some place to stay before it gets dark?" Chris asked.

"We'll stay here," Johnny said, smiling.

"Overnight?" Chris gasped.

"Why not?" her father said. "It's a hotel, isn't it?"

At the wood box, Richard let out a scream and ran with both hands on top of his head. A bat fluttered out of the wood box and circled the room.

Sue and Chris added their screams and joined Richard in running around wildly, hands over their heads, as the bat continued to circle.

"It's only a bat!" Johnny said, trying to be heard above the screams. He opened the front door, the bat flew out, and he slammed it shut.

In the kitchen he found his family huddled in a corner. Sue stood armed with a blackened frying pan, ready to ward off the creature's attack.

"It's gone," Johnny said. "It was more scared than we were. It was only a bat. They can't hurt you."

"Yeah?" Richard said. "In South America they kill whole herds of cattle. They suck their blood —"

"Enough!" Chris yelled.

Johnny looked around the room. "Nice big kitchen, isn't it?" he asked no one in particular.

Sue opened the oven door and slammed it shut. "Johnny! There's something in there!"

Johnny reluctantly walked over to the oven. He didn't especially want to face another bat so soon. And he certainly didn't want to see anything worse. But—he *was* the man of the hotel....

He opened the door an inch—two—three. Nothing happened. He bravely opened it a few more inches. Then he bent down and looked inside.

Four sets of eyes looked out at him. He stood up straight and said, "Sorry." Then he carefully closed the door.

"What is it?" Chris asked.

"Raccoons," Johnny said. "Four of them. A family, I guess."

"Do you expect me to cook around four raccoons?" Sue asked.

"I'll get rid of them," Johnny said.

"The way you got rid of Strongheart when Richard brought him home?" Sue was really angry with him now. "Let's get the things out of the car before dark," she said and stormed out of the room.

"I'll see if there's some place to sleep upstairs," Johnny said to her back. "Richard, see if you can get a fire started."

Upstairs, Johnny found the bedrooms cluttered, dusty, and draped with cobwebs, but well furnished. He admired the carved bedposts and the old-fashioned night tables and dressers in each room.

One room had a balcony. He opened the French window and stepped out on it. Just below him his wife and daughter were unloading the luggage from the roof of the car.

He felt a sudden pang of guilt, the first one since he'd heard about his inheritance. "This isn't exactly what I'd had in mind for them," he said to himself.

Then he had a vision of what the lobby of the Grand Imperial might look like after a major cleaning job. He thought of the beautiful old furniture and the old-fashioned feather beds in each of the bedrooms, and immediately felt cheered.

"Hey!" he called out. "Wait till you see what's upstairs!"

At the sound of his father's voice, Richard ran out of the hotel, slamming the door behind him, and this loosened the snow on the roof. Johnny's wife and children looked up toward the balcony in time to see a small avalanche of snow descend on the head of the house.

And when he began to wriggle, because some snow went down his back, he heard laughter from below.

"That's not funny!" he said. Then he looked down. It was the first time in eight gloomy days that he'd seen them laughing. "Well," he added, "maybe it is funny, at that."

Suddenly he grabbed a handful of snow, packed it into a ball, and threw it at his audience. Sue put down the suitcase she was carrying and made a snowball of her own. She tossed it his way, and he ducked just it time.

Soon it was a general free-for-all. Strongheart joined in by chasing around after snowballs and barking joyfully.

Johnny watched the scene from the balcony. "It's going to be all right," he thought. "It's going to work. I *know* it is."

Dinner that night was informal. Johnny offered to drive back into town to get some food, but the others vetoed that idea. It was already dark, and nobody was sure he'd be able to find his way back.

So they made a meal of leftovers collected at their various motel stops: pretzels, potato chips, a couple of oranges, some grapes, and three cans of cola.

At nine o'clock, Johnny suggested that they go to bed. No one complained. They took a pile of sheets from a suitcase and made up three beds using mothball-smelling blankets they found folded up in bureau drawers. Johnny found some candles and holders in a cabinet.

Before turning in, Sue went to check on Richard and Chris. Both were sound alseep, so she went down the hall to her bedroom.

Johnny was under the covers, his hands behind his head, staring at the ceiling. He was not alone, however. The faithful Strongheart lay across Sue's side of the bed.

"Off," she said.

Strongheart reacted in his usual way. He ignored her.

"Off!" she repeated.

Nothing. Sue put her candle on the night table and got to work dragging him off the bed. Strongheart didn't exactly resist; he just lay there, all 200 pounds of him.

"Give me a hand here," she said.

Johnny pushed from his side. Strongheart stared straight ahead, as though he had no idea what they were trying to do. But when they got him to the edge of the bed, he suddenly gave in, hopped to the floor, and padded over to a corner. There he curled up, ready for sleep.

"I thought you'd appreciate the warm spot," Johnny said. He'd returned to staring at the ceiling.

"It isn't worth all that work," she said, climbing under the covers.

She lay her head down and sighed. "It's been a long, long day," she said. Then she turned and looked at Johnny. He seemed to be considering some cosmic riddle that was written on the ceiling.

"Worried?" she asked.

"Yep."

"We still have $1,700. We can stretch that a long way." He didn't say anything. "We *do* have $1,700, don't we?"

"The lawyer's fee was $1,000," he said.

Sue sat up and looked down at him. "You gave them $1,000 to get yourself legally stuck with this rundown igloo?"

"It's all in his letter," Johnny said. "Title search, transfer deed, a dozen other things."

She put her head back down next to his. "You have good reason to worry," she said.

Now the two of them stared at the ceiling. The only sound they could hear was Strongheart's heavy breathing. Sue considered blowing out the candle, but she was too relaxed to move.

Then they heard a thump.

"What's that?" Sue asked, sitting upright.

"I think it was from downstairs." Johnny hopped out of bed.

"Probably the raccoons," Sue said hopefully. Then they heard a loud slam.

"I don't want to see the raccoon that can do that!" Johnny said, heading for the door.

"Wait! Take Strongheart with you!"

Johnny looked over at Strongheart. The world's worst watchdog was pretending to be asleep.

"I don't need a 200-pound chicken with me," Johnny said. "I might trip over him."

"Take him!" Sue hopped out of bed and went over and prodded Strongheart.

The great dog sighed. Slowly he lifted himself and followed his master into the hallway.

The thumping was getting louder. It was loud enough to wake Chris and Richard, who came out to see what it was. Johnny stood at the head of the stairs with a candle in his hand.

"Is someone trying to break in?" Chris asked.

"Maybe some*thing*!" Richard said.

Sue joined them in the hall. "It sounds like it's coming from the kitchen," she said.

Johnny put his hand on Strongheart's head. "Let's go, boy," he said.

"Dad?" Richard said. "If you really want me to, I'll go with you." The shakiness in his voice made it clear what he hoped his father would say.

"Take this," Johnny said, handing Richard the candle. "Stay here with your mother and Chris."

When he reached the foot of the stairs, Johnny realized that the banging noise was the slamming of cupboard doors in the kitchen. He tiptoed in that direction, dragging Strongheart by the scruff of the neck.

Standing in the kitchen doorway, Johnny could hear someone — something? — moving around, as the banging continued. It was too dark to see anything. He inched toward the stove, holding onto Strongheart's neck all the time.

He felt around the top of the stove for the box of wooden matches. He found one and struck it on the top of the stove.

The sudden light surprised a large, furry creature that had stuck its head in the oven. It roared from inside the oven, and then the creature began to straighten up. It was enormous!

Johnny stepped back and dropped the match. Strongheart padded for the stairs. In the dark kitchen, the creature seemed to head for the doorway. There was a sound of breaking glass, and a grunt as the creature moved out to the lobby.

Johnny struck another match, lit a candle, and followed the creature. There was another roar, followed by distinct words.

"Pea-brained meddler!" the creature bellowed. "Where are you?"

Holding the candle in front of him, Johnny saw an ancient looking man wearing a ratty fur coat that reached to his shoes.

"Look what you done!" the man yelled. He went back to the lobby entrance and stared sadly down at the liquid and glass remains of a pint bottle.

"She was almost full," he said mournfully. Johnny stared at him in disbelief.

"I stashed her there last summer," the old man said, "just for a night like this one. Now there ain't a sniff left." His voice started rising again. "Of all the jingle-brained jackasses! You don't know split beans from coffee, comin' up on a person like that!"

"Me?" Johnny said, annoyed and amused at the same time. "You're the one who did the scaring! Who are you, and what are you doing in my hotel?"

"*Your* hotel?" The anger drained from his face, and he now looked interested. "Oh, you the new honcho around here?"

"This is my property, if that's what you mean." Johnny hadn't meant to sound that stuffy, but it was out before he could stop it. "And I'd like to know what some stranger is doing roaming around my kitchen."

"Stranger, is it? I'm no stranger, Mister. Name's Jesse McCord. Jake used to help me out when times were bad. He let me winter here for the last 50 years. Soon as I made my strike, we was gonna split right down the middle."

"Well, my name's Baxter, and things are different now. If you want a room, we have plenty to rent."

"Oh? How much you get for a bed?"

Johnny had no idea how much he would get for a bed. But he couldn't let this old coot think he didn't know how to run his own hotel. He put on his best professional hotel-owner's voice.

"Uh — ten dollars." Jesse tilted his head and studied him. "In advance," Johnny added.

"In advance!"

"Right," Johnny said crisply, enjoying his first hotel business deal.

An hour later, they all sat around the fire Chris and Richard had built in the largest fireplace. Jesse had donated some coffee from his camping gear, and Sue had persuaded Johnny to brew a pot.

Jesse had won them over with stories of

Jake, the old silver mines, and the days when Silver Hill had been a booming mining town.

"In those days," he said, "$14,000 a month weren't nothing. Jake was still taking in that much a month after the last mine ran empty."

"How long ago was that?" Richard asked.

"Long before you was born," Jesse said, sipping his coffee. He looked Johnny up and down. "In fact, it was probably long before your daddy was born, too."

Sue smiled at Johnny, who didn't feel her reaction was appropriate. He frowned back at her.

"Well," Jesse said, putting his cup down, "about time for me to be going. Makes me real happy to see nice folks like yourselves taking over Jake's place."

He struggled into his coat, which seemed to weigh a little more than he did.

"This place has been like home to me," Jesse went on, looking around the room. Then he began coughing. Between coughs, he managed to say, "Listen to that wind, will you?"

"Johnny?" Sue said.

Johnny looked at her. Jesse's little playlet brought a slight smile to his lips.

"Johnny, maybe you can drive him into town."

"Why, bless your heart, ma'am," Jesse

said. His cough had disappeared. "That's awful sweet of you. But there's no point going into town when I have no place to stay. No, I'll find me a hollow tree or something, and I'll be fine."

He began collecting his camping gear. Johnny smirked as his wife and the children looked from him to the old man and back again. Then Jesse stood before him, hardly visible behind the coat and the gear.

"Mr. Baxter, sir," he said, "if we don't meet again in this world, I want you to know it's been an honor just being with you and your wonderful family for a spell."

"Dad..." Chris said.

"Come on, Dad," Richard added.

Sue stared at Johnny, waiting.

Johnny sighed. "All right. He can stay." Chris and Richard smiled. "But he's going to have to work, like the rest of us."

Jesse's gear was on the floor, and he was already half out of his coat. "I'm no stranger to work, Mr. Baxter," he said. "I'll be the best bartender you ever had."

Johnny remembered the solemn tone Jesse had used when he'd talked about the broken bottle. He shook his head slowly at the old man.

"Bellhop," he said.

Jesse shrugged. "Bellhop it is," he said.

Chris and Richard picked up his gear. "Come on," Richard said. "You can have the corner room."

Sue and Johnny watched them go up the stairs. "We got ourselves a bellhop," she said. "Cheap."

Their children bounded up the stairs with his gear. Jesse took the stairs one at a time, very, very slowly. He turned and smiled at his new employers.

"Somehow," Johnny whispered, "bell*hop* sounds a bit optimistic for what we've got."

Johnny drove into town the next morning and bought about half the stock on the shelves of the grocery store. At least it seemed that way. There were really no supplies at the hotel; everything needed to be bought.

So Johnny piled the grocery counter high with food to get them through the week — things like eggs, bread, soup, and other edibles. And he also had to buy all the basic things you need to run a house — staples like flour and sugar, and supplies like soap, napkins, toothpaste.

Johnny also stopped at the hardware store for tools they'd need to make repairs and start the remodeling work — hammers and nails, a set of screwdrivers, three crowbars, an electric drill, and a sander.

The hotel had several sets of dishes, glasses, and hotel silverware, so that was one expense they could dodge. There were also plenty of towels, sheets, and pillow cases.

These were yellowed with age, and wouldn't be of much use until they could get a washing machine.

By ten o'clock, breakfast was over, and everybody was hard at work. Chris and Richard were dusting and polishing the furniture in the lobby. It took them a long time, because as soon as they finished rubbing a chair leg or a table top, they'd step back and admire their work. Still, it made it a little easier to believe that the place would someday look really good.

Sue was cleaning out the fireplaces, a job for which she had volunteered. "I haven't cleaned one of these things since I was 14," she'd said. "That was the last time I spent the summer at my grandmother's."

Johnny used a crowbar to take the boards off the windows. He was happy to find that most of the windows were in good shape. All they needed was a paint job.

Jesse was helping Johnny. At least, he held the rickety old ladder whenever Johnny had to reach the top of a window. Actually, he was keeping Johnny company, and getting a chance to talk to a willing audience after months of solitude.

Jesse continued the narrative that had been

interrupted the night before. He had 50 years of stories to fill them in on, and Johnny didn't mind listening a bit.

"Oh, $14,000 a month was peanuts in those days," said Jesse, holding the ladder while Johnny eased the crowbar behind a board. "Course, we had day sleepers and night sleepers then. You'd rent a bed for $20 for eight hours. Then they'd get the room ready for the next shift."

Johnny got down from the ladder. He went to work on the bottom part of the board. Jesse moved the ladder to the next window.

"Jake was riding high in those days," he went on. "Then the mines played out, the customers stopped coming, and finally the town all but closed down. The Grand Imperial started downhill. But Jake never gave up. He always said the good days would be back. He was just going through some bad times."

Johnny pried the board from the window and let a little more sunlight into the room. Chris and Richard looked up from their work, pleased with the added brightness.

"Why did they call him Crazy Jake?" Johnny asked.

"Aw, *that*," Jesse said, dismissing the nickname with a small wave of his hand.

"Jake was playing with a full deck, believe me. Everybody who really knew him knew that."

"Then why the nickname?" Johnny asked.

"He was just different from most folks. Like, he'd always have some kind of bird in here with a busted wing. When the snow got deep, he'd leave food out for the deer. He couldn't stand to see anybody hurting, people or animals. When the hard times hit the Injuns, he took care of a lot of them."

Sue picked up her bucket of water and went behind the bar to refill it. She turned on the tap, but nothing happened.

"Johnny," she called, "the water's stopped up."

"Wait a few seconds," Jesse said. "It's probably one of them guppies stuck in there."

He was right. The water suddenly burst forth into the bucket.

"It's a fish!" Sue cried. Johnny, Chris, and Richard rushed up to look.

"That's what I was saying," Jesse said. "They get sucked up out of the pond."

"There's *fish* in the sink water?" Chris said.

"Can't hurt you none," Jesse said. "They're just curious little fellers. Jake used to get a kick out of seeing them come out. 'Dropping in for a visit' is what he always called it. He'd put them all in a bucket or something and bring them back to the pond at the end of the day."

"Oh, no," Sue said. "Johnny —"

"Now, don't worry," Johnny said. "I'll get it fixed."

"When?" she asked. "Or should I ask — with *what*?"

"Well," Johnny said, "uh —"

"This morning's shopping," Sue said, "has already put a dent in what little money we had."

"I know," Johnny said. "Well, I'll — uh — I'll get a loan somewhere!"

"You caught *me* at a bad time," Jesse said. "I haven't had any spare cash since before the Great Depression."

"No, no, I mean a *bank* loan," Johnny said. He turned and made a sweeping gesture of the lobby.

"A lot of things need fixing around here," he said, and indicated *what* things by using the crowbar as a pointer. "Some of the furniture has to be repaired. A few broken windows. We could use some new carpeting."

Johnny let the crowbar drop with a clang. "Sure, that's what we'll do!" he said enthusiastically. "Jesse, is there a bank in town?"

"Bank of Silver Hill," Jesse said. "Owned by a man named Ridgeway." The tone of his voice and the look on his face plainly showed that he thought Ridgeway was a snake-in-the-grass.

"Ridgeway?" Johnny said. "Sue, that's the guy who's interested in buying this place. That means he must think it's worth the investment. And *that* means he'll lend us the money!"

"How much money you going to get, Dad?" Richard asked.

"Well, I don't know. I'll get enough to do the job right, though. If we're going to run a hotel, let's run a first-class hotel. Right?"

"Right!" Richard and Chris said together.

"Right!" Jesse added.

Off in a corner, Strongheart barked once. Johnny looked at Sue, waiting for her vote. She smiled, took a deep breath, and said, softly, "Right." They all cheered. "I hope," she added, under her breath.

All Johnny knew about Ridgeway was that he owned the local bank and he was interested in Johnny's property. Everyone in town, including Jesse, knew a lot more than that. But Jesse liked Johnny and didn't want to ruin his dream. He was sure that Johnny would soon see what Ridgeway was up to.

When Martin Ridgeway was five years old, he had a friend named Willie in nursery school. Willie moved away the following year. He was the last friend Martin Ridgeway ever had.

In first grade, he'd steal other kids' lunches and throw them away. Then he'd offer to sell bits of his own lunch at ridiculously high prices.

At seven, he sold newspapers on a street corner. He got them free, because they were yesterday's papers. He got away with that for several weeks.

With schemes like these, Ridgeway grew up to be a very sharp real estate dealer. Eventually, he started his own bank, and by now, he owned almost every piece of property in and around Silver Hill.

At 50, Ridgeway had more money — and more property — than he would ever need. But still he wanted more. He would always want more. It didn't matter that he didn't *need* more property. He *wanted* it. And one of the properties he wanted most of all was the Grand Imperial Hotel.

Johnny didn't know any of this, of course. He went to the bank, smiling and happy, with not the slightest suspicion that Ridgeway was out to kill Johnny's chances of success with the hotel. As Ridgeway read Johnny's loan application, he maintained a carefully blank, poker-playing expression. He had already listened with the same poker face to Johnny's plan for remodeling the place and running it as a family hotel. Now Johnny sat silent, nervously watching Ridgeway's face for some sign, but there was none.

Finally, Ridgeway looked up from the application and down at Johnny.

The applicant's chair was purposely set four inches lower than Ridgeway's to make the applicant feel at a disadvantage immediately.

He held the application out in front of him, opened his fingers, and let it float to the desk. Then he sighed and shook his head.

"I'm afraid not, Mr. Baxter," he said. "Your hotel is too big a risk for my bank."

Johnny's shoulders sagged. He swallowed hard and said, "But why, Mr. Ridgeway?"

"Several reasons. It isn't centrally located. The facilities are sub-standard. And your current assets—" He looked down at the application and smirked. "Well, let's say your assets leave something to be desired."

"But it has great potential, Mr. Ridgeway. It just needs a little fixing up."

"Mr. Baxter, have you ever managed a hotel?"

"Well, no, but—"

"Have you ever run a restaurant? Supervised employees?"

"No, but it shouldn't be too hard to learn. I mean, the beds are all there, and the dishes and linens, and Sue's a great cook."

Ridgeway sighed again and lifted himself from his great chair. "I'd like to help you, Baxter," he said. "But as president of this bank, I have a responsibility to our depositors."

He was on his way to the door of his office. Johnny stood and jumped in his way.

"But you offered to buy the place yourself!" He reached in his pocket and took out the letter Mr. Fowler had given him.

"Yes," Ridgeway said, stepping around him. "The offer still stands."

"I don't understand," Johnny said, as Ridgeway opened the office door and stepped out into the bank.

"Explain it to me," Johnny said, following him out. "If it isn't good business for the bank, why is it good business for you?"

Miss Wiggington, Ridgeway's secretary, looked up from her typing, as eager to hear her boss's answer as Johnny was.

"My interest, Mr. Baxter, is not a business one," Ridgeway said.

"Not business?"

"No, Mr. Baxter. You see, I'm a sentimentalist. Your uncle was a fine old gentleman. A lot of people didn't understand him, but I — excuse me."

Ridgeway seemed overcome with emotion. He took out a handkerchief and dabbed at his eyes. Miss Wiggington watched in amazement. This was one of the best performances she'd ever seen her boss give.

Back in control of himself, Ridgeway went on. "Jacob Barnsworth was a true humanitarian. It is my intention to refurbish his hotel and turn it into something that will honor his memory as it should be honored. Mr. Baxter, I want that property to become known as The Jacob Barnsworth Home for Wayward Boys!"

Miss Wiggington had to turn back to her typing at that point. Unless she got her mind back on her work she would surely explode with indignation — or rude laughter.

"Home for wayward boys?" Johnny said sheepishly. "Well, that would be very nice. I mean, for the memory of Uncle Jake and all."

"So I'm willing to take it off your hands, Baxter. I can have the papers drawn up before the end of the day."

"Well, thanks, Mr. Ridgeway. But — uh — I'd have to talk it over with my wife first."

"Of course, young man, of course! It's just that I think we should all do something for our fellow man while we can." Ridgeway was guiding Johnny to the street door. "But don't let my sentimental intentions influence you one bit. If you're set on going ahead with this wild scheme, I'd be the last person to discourage you."

At the door, Johnny smiled weakly at

Ridgeway. "Thanks, Mr. Ridgeway," he said. "I'm glad you see it that way."

"Let me know what you decide to do," Ridgeway said, pushing Johnny out the door. "And while you're trying to decide, keep in mind two important things. You have no experience. And you have no capital. Good day."

The door closed in Johnny's face. Ridgeway strode back to his office. He stopped in front of Miss Wiggington's desk.

She looked up at him and said merely, "The Jacob Barnsworth Home for Wayward Boys?"

Ridgeway chuckled. "If that fool knew what that property was worth —"

As he went into his office and closed the door behind him, the chuckle turned into a cackle.

Two sets of footprints in the snow trailed from the hotel in an uneven path up to the top of the hill. At the end of the trail, Johnny and Sue stood looking back at what might have been a new start for them.

"Maybe it's all for the best," Sue said. "Maybe we'd be just throwing good money after bad."

They went on walking, their hands buried deep in the pockets of their ski coats.

"For a while there," Johnny said, "I actually thought we could make it work. We could have written to friends, convinced them to vacation up here. They'd tell their friends, and we'd be in business. We'd never get rich, maybe, but it would have been a good life. And not only for the kids. For us, too. I kind of like it up here."

Sue put her arm around his waist. "Me too," she confessed. "Raccoons and all."

They walked on in silence, each day-dreaming about what it might have been like. From far off, they heard a whirring sound, as though some crazed gardener was running a lawn mower. The sound got louder. Then they saw a snowmobile heading their way.

As it got closer, they could see that it was a patchwork affair, put together from what remained of several wrecks. No two pieces of the vehicle fit together exactly, and it carried eight or ten different colors of paint. The machine stopped right in front of them, and a driver in crash helmet and goggles got out.

"Hi!" he said. "Taking a walk in the snow?"

Johnny and Sue smiled. The question didn't seem to call for an answer. The driver stood looking at them, waiting for them to say something. When he spoke, he sounded a little surprised.

"Don't you remember me?" he asked. Then he realized they couldn't see him. He removed the helmet and goggles. "Wally Perkins. From the gas station?"

"Oh, sure," Sue said. "Good to see you."

Johnny was walking around the snowmobile, trying to figure out what held it together. Wally noticed, and laughed.

"It doesn't look like much," he said, "but it

runs. It used to be four snowmobiles — five, counting the motor. They got totaled in last year's Cross Country, and I collected the pieces."

"What's the Cross Country?" Sue asked.

"The Silver Hill Annual Cross Country Snowmobile Race. Folks around here hold it every year."

"Cross country?" Johnny said. "Must be pretty rough."

"You bet!" Wally said. "It gets hairy sometimes! Martin Ridgeway's won it the last three years."

He looked down the hill in the direction of the hotel. "Uh, how's the family?" he asked.

"Fine," Sue said. "Chris is in the kitchen. Why don't you go down and say hello?"

"Good idea," Wally said, as though that hadn't been the reason he came in the first place. He put on his helmet and goggles again. "Hope you don't mind me making tracks in your snow."

Johnny looked over the white expanse surrounding him, as Wally climbed back into his machine, and his face lit up.

"Hey, wait!" he called to Wally. "You said, 'in your snow.' *My* snow.?"

"Sure," Wally said.

"Is this *all* my snow?"

"I guess so. If you want it."

"Sue," Johnny said, "didn't Jesse say the property went back into those hills?"

"I wasn't listening."

"It does," Wally said. "It goes as far as you can see."

"And all that beautiful, precious snow is ours," Johnny said, beaming.

"Around here," Wally said, "you can't get much for snow, Mr. Baxter."

"Johnny," Sue said, "what's going on?"

"What's the most popular sport in the country right now?" Johnny asked.

"Baseball?" she said.

"No, no, not spectator sport. Where do the Feiffers go every weekend? And Roy and Barbara?"

Sue's eyes widened as she said, "Skiing."

"Right! And half the time they complain because they can't find a place to stay."

"A ski lodge?" Sue said, as her face turned red with excitement.

"Look at that hill!" Johnny said, pointing. "People will come from all over the country to ski a hill like that!"

"But —" Sue started, then stopped. Then she realized they *had* to talk about it. "It would cost a fortune to start something like that."

"Sure, but Ridgeway would be glad to lend us money on this!"

"Don't bet on it," Wally said from the sidelines.

"Okay," Johnny said, almost yelling now. "Then I'll go to another bank. How about Crystal Highlands? They have banks there, don't they?"

"Sure," Wally said, losing interest in whatever it was they were talking about. He climbed into his snowmobile, started it up, and called, "See you later!"

"Just look at it!" Johnny sang out. "Have you ever seen a skiing site like this one?"

Johnny hung up the phone and grinned at his family. "Mr. Walter Wainwright," he said, "of the Crystal Highlands National Bank wants to meet me this afternoon."

He waited a few seconds for the cheering to die down. Then he said, "I'm meeting him at the ski shop."

"Why the ski shop?" Richard asked.

"He's a skiing nut himself. That's probably why he's interested."

"You mean you're going to ski with him, Dad?" Chris asked.

"Wally," Johnny said, "do you have some skis and ski clothes I can borrow?"

"Sure," Wally said.

"Johnny!" Sue said. "You don't know a thing about skiing. Besides, you get nervous going down an escalator!"

"Sue," Johnny told her patiently, "you can't expect a bank to lend money for a ski lodge to someone who doesn't ski."

"But — "

"It's better if he thinks I know what I'm doing. I made that mistake with Ridgeway when I admitted I knew nothing about the hotel business. I'm not making the same mistake twice."

"Johnny — " Sue said.

"Don't worry, honey. I'll get out of it somehow. Move over Crystal Highlands! Make way for the Grand Imperial Ski Lodge!"

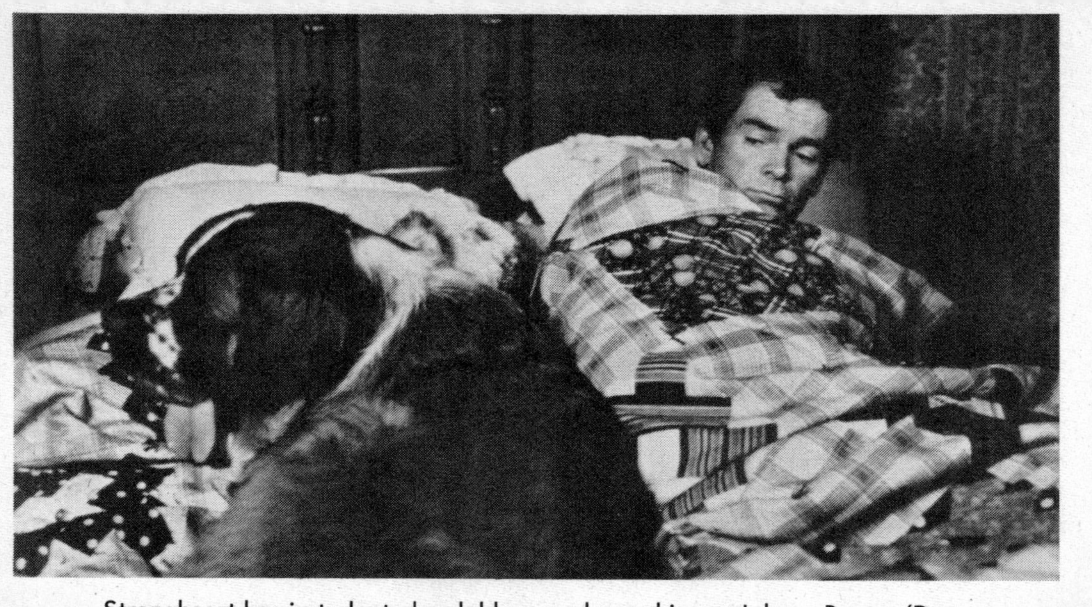

Strongheart has just planted a slobbery wake-up kiss on Johnny Baxter (Dean Jones). This is the day Johnny will inherit a hotel in Colorado.

The Baxters' first night in their Colorado hotel is disturbed by strange noises in the kitchen. Here, Johnny investigates the "furry animal."

To turn the hotel into a ski lodge, Johnny needs money. To impress banker Wainwright (George Kirkpatrick) with his skiing ability, he faces a heart-stopping ski run — but Johnny can't ski!

Two views of a would-be ski-lodge owner, on skis for the first time!

Crafty old Ridgeway (Keenan Wynn) is counting on Johnny's inexperience. (above) He offers Johnny and Sue (Nancy Olson) a short-term bank loan. (below) Johnny and Sue need $25,000; Ridgeway offers $3,000. "I'll take it," says Johnny.

Johnny and Sue have learned to ski — a *little*. Here they joyously survey their property.

Wally (Michael Greevey), a willing if inexperienced "helper," has succeeded in exploding a tree stump. The watchers — Johnny and Sue Baxter, Richard and Chris Baxter (Johnny Whitaker and Kathleen Cody), and handyman Jesse McCord (Harry Morgan) — will soon feel the effects of the explosion. It causes a nearby avalanche — and a business boom for them.

Wally's ski instruction comes fresh from the ski manual. Here he shares his "crash course" with his pupil, Miss Grable (Judy Drummer).

Alas! Wally's ski demonstration takes him down and over the cliff. Hang in there, boy!

Jesse is doing his bit. He's moving the ancient donkey engine into place to ferry skiers up the slope in a makeshift towline. Will it work?

The donkey engine works fine — only Jesse can't stop it or steer it. He has just passed through one wall of the hotel — now he's headed for the other side!

Richard, Chris, Wally, and Jesse close ranks with Sue and Johnny when Ridgeway comes to take over the hotel. Will Ridgeway acquire this property, too? Not if his secretary can help it!

Johnny stood in front of the Crystal Highlands Ski Shop, trying his best to look as though he was glad he was there. Wally's ski outfit almost fit him, though the sleeves were a bit short, and the waistband on the pants did make him regret all those potato chips he'd had the night before.

He had just walked from the parking lot to the entrance to the ski shop. It hadn't been easy, carrying his (Wally's) skis. He had managed to scrape the fenders of two parked cars, knock down a directional sign, and cut his left thumb, trying to balance the slithery things. As he stood in front of the shop, he watched the other skiers. They moved gracefully, carrying their skis snugly on their shoulders.

In imitation, Johnny hoisted his skis to his shoulders. Then he turned to see if he could find Mr. Wainwright — and banged the ski tips against the shop window.

Fortunately, before more pre-ski events could take place, a man came up to him and said, "Mr. Baxter?"

"Yes. Mr. Wainwright?"

"Good to see you," Wainwright said, offering his hand. "If you don't mind, I thought we could talk on the way up."

"Up?" Johnny said blankly.

"In the chair lift," Wainwright said, leading Johnny by the arm. "There's almost no line at this time of day, and I knew you wouldn't want to waste the opportunity."

Johnny saw that Wainwright was not a skier to be distracted, and followed him to the lift. There he saw the skiers hop, two by two, into each chair as it came to the station. Then he looked up at where the chairs were headed.

The top of the ski lift wasn't what scared Johnny. At the top, the skiers at least had some solid ground under their feet—even if it was covered with soft snow. It was the airy distance between where the chair lift started up and the top that made Johnny think he might try patching things up with Mr. Carruthers, back in the New York office.

He watched one of the chairs rising higher and higher up the lift, noting how the distance steadily increased between the skiers' feet and the ground, and his stomach lurched. It reminded Johnny of the way he'd often felt when he'd looked down from his tenth-floor office window at Indemnity and Casualty.

Only a few people were lined up ahead of them, and Johnny realized he'd be in one of those chairs in a matter of minutes — maybe seconds if everything went wrong. He kept trying to swallow, without any luck. Maybe a sudden avalanche would save him.

"One quick descent," Mr. Wainwright said cheerfully, "and we can get down to lunch and business." He smiled at Johnny.

Johnny smiled back and tried to make his voice sound as though it weren't coming from the bottom of a cave. "Nothing like one quick descent before lunch," he said brightly.

Wainwright was so intent on having a good time that he paid little attention to his companion. This gave Johnny the chance to watch what Wainwright did and imitate it all, a few seconds behind at each step.

They eased their way into position for the next chair. Johnny was working so hard at making his imitation believable, trying to hold his body in just the right way (the Wainwright way), that the chair moved in behind them and scooped them up before he realized what was happening.

Johnny let out a cry of surprise, and several skiers looked up at him, startled.

"What was that?" Wainwright asked.

"That?" Johnny said, trying to seat himself comfortably in the chair. "Oh, that was just—uh—singing! I get so carried away up here, I feel like singing sometimes."

"I know just what you mean," Wainwright said. "I'm glad to see that kind of enthusiasm. A man with that kind of feel for skiing is a man I like doing business with."

"Well," Johnny said, "no sense going into any business without enthusia — " He cut himself short when he happened to look down.

He was now gliding farther off the ground than he had ever been before in his life. Worse, when he looked up he found he still had a long, long way to go. The chair was rising and swaying in the wind, swaying and rising.

Johnny threw his head back as far as he could. If he looked down again, he knew he'd get dizzy, perhaps even faint! But he had this uncontrollable urge to look down.

"Is something wrong?" Wainwright asked.

"Wrong?" Johnny repeated, keeping his head back. "Oh, you mean the way I'm sitting? No, nothing's wrong. I just like to get the full force of the sun when I'm on the way up."

Wainwright seemed satisfied by that. "Some of the skiers call this run Nightmare Alley," he said. "But I think you'll enjoy it."

Johnny continued to stare at the sky. Wainwright whistled "Up, Up, and Away" for a while, until he began to lose the melody.

Then he said, "Do you plan to do your own instructing?"

Johnny had become so engrossed in keeping his eyes off the ground that everything else had faded from his mind. "Instructing?" he thought. "What is this man talking about? In fact *who* is this man?"

"Do you?" Wainwright repeated.

The spell passed, and Johnny remembered where he was and why. "Instructing?" he said. "Oh, yes, well, that's one idea we've considered."

He sat upright and made the mistake of looking down. The vast gap between him and the ground made his head spin. He had visions of himself sailing through space, his skis waving crazily over his head. Just as he was about to pass out, the chair jolted and Wainwright hopped off.

Johnny followed him and planted his own skis on the ground. He was panting, but Wainwright didn't notice. He was already on his way to the starting area.

Johnny followed him slowly. "Nightmare Alley," he thought, as they approached the ramp.

They stood together at the starting point. Johnny watched Wainwright adjust his goggles and wrap his pole straps around his wrists.

Wainwright turned to him and said, "Ready?"

"It's now or never," Johnny thought. He grabbed his knee and moaned.

"What's wrong?" Wainwright asked.

"Nothing," Johnny said, holding his knee. "Just an old football injury. Sometimes, if I twist it the wrong way, I — ooooh!"

Wainwright took off his goggles. "We'd better wait a while before we make the run," he said.

"No, no, that's all right," Johnny said quickly. "I don't want to ruin your skiing. You just go ahead. I'll go down slowly and meet you at the bottom."

"Are you sure?" Wainwright asked. He seemed genuinely concerned, and Johnny began to feel a little guilty.

"Please," Johnny said, "go ahead. This happens every once in a while. I'll be okay."

"All right," Wainwright said. "See you later. Be careful." He shoved off down the hill.

As soon as Wainwright was out of sight, Johnny began inching away from the ramp. He had to find some way of getting down. And it had to be considerably less insane than following Wainwright.

Trying to inch up the hill, he had his back to the slope. He caught the eye of two passing skiers. Maybe they could tell him how to do this.

He lifted his pole to wave at them. "Excuse me!" he called.

The movement of his arm caused him to lose his balance. Before the skiers could answer him, he was on his way down the hill—backwards.

"Wait a minute!" he called. As he picked up speed, he waved his arms. He looked as though he hoped to fly out of his predicament and sail to the bottom like a graceful bird.

Wainwright was doing a fancy zigzag pattern on his way down the hill. Moving in a straight line, Johnny soon caught up with him.

"Baxter!" Wainwright called. "You're skiing backwards!"

"Sure!" Johnny yelled. "Takes the strain off the old knee!"

Wainwright watched as Johnny bore down on a woman involved in her own zigzag pattern. As he bounced off the woman, she fell into the snow and he turned around.

"Sorry, ma'am!" Johnny screamed. "I couldn't help myself!"

He was facing forward now. He realized this should be considered an improvement over his condition of a few seconds earlier. But he just couldn't seem to think of it that way, because now he could *see* what was in store for him.

What was in store was the end of solid ground. He was fast approaching an overhanging lip. Because of the angle of his approach, he couldn't see what was beyond it. All he could be sure of was that he was about to leave the ground at a speed he had never imagined before.

"Wait a minute!" he called again, flailing his arms even more wildly.

What he couldn't see was that the lip was only about three feet from the ground beneath it. He also couldn't see the skier bending down in front of it, tightening his ski straps.

As Johnny came flying off the ledge, the skier began to straighten up. Johnny put a stop to that by sliding right over his back. The skier fell face first into the snow.

He zoomed past a group of skiers resting in the snow. They saw what he was doing, but they didn't quite understand. When he hit a snow mound and went into a somersault, they applauded his trick skiing.

Zooming ahead, he crashed through a group of novice skiers, who found themselves suddenly sitting in the snow.

"How do I stop!" he yelled. A second later, he had his answer.

A horse-drawn sleigh was crossing the slope as Johnny burned his way down. The driver, seeing what was about to happen, tried frantically to get the horse to move. But the animal was too interested in the skier bearing down on him.

As he reached the horse, Johnny doubled over just in time. He went sliding under the horse's belly, and the animal shifted his gaze to watch the skier depart.

The doubling up had done the trick. Johnny lost his balance, tumbled over on his side, and slid along for another 40 or 50 feet. He shifted his weight to his back and held his head and legs up in the air.

By the time he came to a stop, he had a huge pillow of snow behind his head. His skis stuck out in the air over him, moving back and forth as though they had a life of their own.

Johnny looked up the hill and saw many, many angry people making fists in his direction. Most of them were saying something or other, but Johnny couldn't hear any of it.

He rested his head on the pillow he'd made. He stilled the flailing skis. Then he breathed a sigh.

"I wonder," he said out loud, "how one goes about finding a banker whose hobby is stamp-collecting."

◇ ◇ 10 ◇ ◇

Johnny was stretched out on the sofa, a large bandage around the top of his head. Sue poured a cup of tea for him and one for herself. Richard sat on the floor near the fireplace, reading aloud from a newspaper.

"The Ski Patrol," Richard read, "had to recruit volunteers to remove Baxter's victims from the slopes. A spokesman at the hospital said they had not treated this many accident cases in one day since the avalanche of 1946."

He put the paper down and looked up at his father, smiling. "Gee, Dad . . . "

"We don't need to hear any more of that," Sue said. She bent down and took the paper from Richard, straightened up, and tossed it into the fireplace.

Then, turning to Johnny, she smiled brightly. "It's good for publicity, anyway," she said.

"But not so good for bank loans," he mumbled.

There was a knock at the front door. Johnny lifted his head, and Richard hopped up and ran to answer the door. Johnny recognized Ridgeway's voice.

"Is Mr. Baxter in?"

"Yes," Richard said. "Come on in."

"Mr. Ridgeway," Johnny said, showing his surprise. He led the banker into the room, where Sue was standing, eyeing him closely.

"Good morning, Baxter," Ridgeway said loudly. "I see you made quite — *a hit* — at Crystal Highlands."

He chuckled at his own joke. Johnny managed to smile. Richard and Strongheart stood in the doorway, and Sue's look had become outright suspicious.

"This must be Mrs. Baxter," Ridgeway said.

"Yes," Sue said coldly. "And this is my son, Richard."

Ridgeway turned to smile down at Richard. "And who is *this*?" he said, pointing to Strongheart.

"Strongheart," Richard said.

"Well, hello there, big fella," Ridgeway said, stepping toward Strongheart.

The growl from the enormous dog was not friendly. Ridgeway stopped.

"Strongheart!" Johnny snapped.

"Richard," Sue said, "put him in the other room."

Richard looked from Strongheart to Ridgeway. "Who?" he asked, genuinely confused.

"Strongheart, that's who!" Johnny said.

Surprised, Richard led the dog toward the kitchen. When they walked past Ridgeway, Richard said, "Dogs are a good judge of character, you know."

When they were gone, Ridgeway sat on a couch. Sue and Johnny sat on chairs opposite him.

"In light of your recent experience," Ridgeway said with a slight smile, "you might want to reconsider my offer to buy this place."

"Thanks, Mr. Ridgeway," Johnny said. "But I think I'll stick with my plans for a ski lodge."

"Is that so?" Ridgeway said. He sounded sincerely impressed at Johnny's determination. Then again, it was impossible to tell when Ridgeway was sincere about anything.

"Tell you what, Baxter," he said. "If you really have your mind set on following your dream, then I'd like to help you make it come true!"

Johnny was stunned. For a few seconds, he

stared at Ridgeway and said nothing. When he finally found his voice, all it produced was, "Really?"

Looking around the room, Ridgeway said, "How much would you need to open the doors in this place?"

This time, Johnny didn't hesitate for a second. "Twenty-five thousand dollars!"

"Good!" Ridgeway said, as though they understood each other perfectly. "I'll lend you three thousand!"

"Well," Sue said, "that should open one door part way."

"I'll take it!" Johnny blurted out.

"Johnny!" Sue gasped.

Ridgeway had taken a contract and a pen from his jacket pocket. "That's the trouble with me," he said smiling broadly. "When my heart and my head disagree, my heart always wins out."

"Johnny," Sue said, "can we talk about this?"

"Not now, Sue."

Ridgeway held the papers and the pen out to Johnny. "I took the liberty of bringing these along," he said. "Just in case. Now, if you'll sign where the check marks are, I can save you a trip into town."

Sue stared in amazement as her husband began signing the papers. Jesse came in, followed by Wally, who was carrying a tool kit.

"Hi, Mrs. Baxter," Wally said pleasantly. "We're gonna take a look at that water heater." Then he saw the banker. "Oh. Hello, Mr. Ridgeway," he said, in a much less friendly tone.

"What are you doing here?" Ridgeway asked.

"Fixing their water heater."

"I thought you were working for Double L."

"I am," Wally said coldly. "This is my day off."

Wally and Jesse walked on into the kitchen. Johnny held the pen and the papers out to Ridgeway, who snatched them from his hands.

Ridgeway took out a checkbook, signed a check, and tore it from the book. Sue noticed that the check had already been made out.

"Here you are, Mr. Baxter. A check for $3,000. Pleasure doing business with you."

Johnny held out his hand to shake with Ridgeway, but the banker was already on his way out the door.

"I'm sure you'll turn the place into something special," he called out. Then he closed the door behind him.

Johnny walked over to Sue and gave her a big hug. "We're in business!" he said.

He didn't seem to notice that she didn't return the hug. He started pacing around the room, rubbing his hands together.

"Let's see, now," he mused, "what'll we need? Make a list, Sue. Let's say five hundred to stock the bar."

He walked toward the kitchen, and Sue followed him. She looked even more worried than she had a few minutes before.

In the kitchen, Wally and Jesse were working on the water heater. Richard sat sulking in the corner, his arm draped over Strongheart's neck. Chris bit into an apple as she watched Wally and Jesse work.

"Johnny," Sue said, "I don't trust that man. He wants this place for something. And it isn't a home for wayward boys."

Johnny smiled as he looked around the kitchen, continuing to make plans in his head. "Don't be so distrustful," he said. "Can't you believe that a rich man like Ridgeway might want to give someone a helping hand?"

Wally looked up from his work. "Not unless he could make a buck at it," he said.

"Here's the proof that he's on our side," Johnny said, waving the check. "He's given us $3,000, hasn't he?"

"He's *lent* us $3,000," Sue said.

"Just like he lent Double L the money to get the garage back on its feet," Wally said.

"There, see?" Johnny said to Sue.

"Only Double L doesn't own the place anymore," Wally said.

"How come?" Johnny asked.

"He fell behind on the payments. Ridgeway took the place over. Now Double L works for him and pays rent on the place."

"That's the same way Babcock lost his place to Ridgeway," Jesse said. "And Pete Bolle. And just about everybody else in these parts."

"Oh, Johnny, what are we getting into?" Sue asked.

"Why is everybody being so pessimistic?" Johnny asked. "All right, so Ridgeway has foreclosed on some property. That's what happens when you can't pay back a loan."

"Sure," Jesse said. "But Ridgeway only seems to lend money to people who can't pay it back."

"Well, then," Johnny said brightly, "he's made a mistake this time. Because we're going to run a ski lodge here that will knock his eyes out!"

"On $3,000?" Chris asked.

"Okay," Johnny said, accepting his daughter's challenge. "Let's figure out what we can do with $3,000."

He opened a drawer and took out a pencil and a small pad. He held them out to Sue, who took them with a look of resignation on her face.

"Write it all down, Sue. I said $500 for the bar, right? Figure another $500 for groceries. We don't want to serve anything but the finest food."

As he talked, he opened and closed cupboard doors, trying to make sure he wouldn't forget anything important.

"Pots, pans, cooking utensils, let's say $300 at the outside. Carpeting, lamps, replace some of the furniture upstairs. Put down $1,200 for that, Sue. What does that all come to?"

"Twenty-five hundred dollars," she said slowly. "You still don't have a ski instructor, and they don't come cheap."

"I do!" Wally said, planting himself in front of her.

"Have you ever been an instructor?" Johnny asked.

"No," Wally said, shrugging. "But if I sew a band on my sleeve, who's going to know the difference?

"Would you work for $100 a month, plus room and board?" Johnny asked.

Wally smiled, more at Chris than at Johnny. "Sure!" he said.

"You mean he's going to live here?" Chris asked. Sue noticed that the annoyance in her daughter's voice didn't sound very convincing.

"You'll double your food budget," Jesse said. "Did you see what he did to that roast last night?"

"That takes care of the ski instructor," Johnny said, walking out into the dining room. Sue followed him out, pad and pencil in hand.

"We'll need more glasses and dishes," Johnny said. "And a few more towels, sheets, and pillow cases. How much do you figure for that stuff, hon?"

Sue shrugged her shoulders. "A couple of hundred dollars, I guess," she said.

"Good. Put that down. How much?"

"That's $2,700."

"Fine," Johnny said, rubbing his hands. "That still leaves us about $300 for a rope tow engine."

He sat on the couch and looked up at Sue, who was standing over him. It was the first time he'd really noticed her since Ridgeway had appeared in their doorway.

"Sue," he said softly, "I know what you think about all this. I know you keep seeing all the pitfalls. Lord knows they're really there to be seen. Come here, please."

He held out his arms. She tossed the pad and pencil on the couch and sat in his lap. He looked up at her face and saw the fear in her eyes.

"I know you'd rather I sold the place to Ridgeway," he said. "But I can't. I just can't. Sue, I've never wanted anything as much as I want this."

"I know," she whispered, touching his cheek. "And I'm not against it. I'm just more scared than you are."

"Try not to be," he said. "Just for a little while longer. Just until we've had a chance to get started."

"I'll try," she said. "But all I can promise is that I'll go along with you. I can't promise not to be scared."

"Let's make a deal," Johnny said. "I'll do whatever I can to keep you from thinking about being scared."

"Okay," she said, smiling. "What do I have to do?"

"You have to keep me from thinking that a $3,000 loan can turn me into an international hotel magnate."

"Count on me for that," she said, kissing him on the forehead.

She hopped from his lap and picked up the pad and pencil. She was already jotting things on the pad when she reached the stairs.

"I'll have a collection of lists for you in an hour or so," she called over her shoulder.

Johnny smiled at the ceiling. "We're off and running," he said aloud. "WE ARE OFF AND RUNNING!" he yelled.

He ran out the door and slammed it behind him. Sue, Richard, Wally, and Jesse came into the room to see what the yelling was about. They found the room empty. They couldn't see Johnny turning cartwheels in the snow.

◇◇ 11 ◇◇

From above, it looked like a white desert covered with tiny diamonds that reflected the light of the midday sun. In the center of this desert stood a huge jewel, the result of the labor of five people, a reluctant St. Bernard, and a $3,000 loan.

The Grand Imperial Hotel had been repainted, repaired, and redecorated. It now stood proudly proclaiming its stature to the surrounding valley. A banner across the wide front entrance announced the GRAND OPENING.

The banner flapped rhythmically in the gentle breeze. The flapping was the only sound to be heard in the valley. Although it was the height of the ski season, not a single customer had answered the ads Johnny and Sue had placed in newspapers and magazines.

Inside the hotel, Richard stood at the kitchen entrance, a dish towel tucked into the front of his pants. The new busboy of the Grand Imperial Hotel was using a rolled-up menu as a telescope to scan the lobby.

He saw his father behind the registration desk, his chin resting in one hand. Johnny's other hand tapped in time to the radio music coming from the overhead speakers.

The telescope moved on to spot Chris, in a waitress uniform, leaning against a wall and tapping her foot. Richard moved his spyglass to the right and found Jesse half asleep in an easy chair. He was the least alert-looking bellhop Richard had ever seen.

Richard got bored with the telescope, unrolled the menu, and put it back on one of the tables. He took a cracker from the basket in the middle of the table and bit into it. The crunching sound was magnified by the dead silence in the room. Jesse, Chris, and Johnny all looked over at him.

"Stop eating the crackers, Richard," Johnny said. His tone suggested that he'd already said the same thing a dozen times.

"There's nobody else here to eat them," Richard said through a mouth full of cracker.

"There'll be plenty of skiers," Johnny said, staring out the window. "As soon as they discover us."

"That's what you said last week," Richard said.

A train whistle in the distance made Jesse look at his watch "There's the 2:50," he said, "loaded with big-tipping skiers." Then he closed his eyes and added, "All headed for Crystal Highlands."

Sue came in with a pot of hot coffee. "Mom," Richard said, "can I go help Wally?"

"No," she said, putting the pot down. "I don't want you around those explosives."

"But Wally knows all about explosives!"

"Maybe he does," Sue said. "But you don't."

Chris glanced out the window, a worried look on her face. "Shouldn't he have that stump out by now?" she asked.

"Don't fret, sweetheart," Jesse said, without opening his eyes. "You'll know when the stump is out."

As if to prove Jesse's point, an enormous explosion rocked the building and everyone in it. Great clumps of loosened snow fell past the windows from the roof.

The explosion was still echoing through the hills when Chris and Richard ran to the window, just in time to see something flying into the sky.

"Is that the stump?" Richard asked in awe.

"If it isn't," Jesse said, "we're gonna be in the market for a new ski instructor."

The distant whistle gave another call. Then it gave another, and another, and another. From the hotel window they could see Wally reacting to the sound. He jumped into his snowmobile and drove off.

Seconds later, he was back in view, speeding toward the hotel. By the time he reached the entrance, everyone was out front waiting for him.

He turned off the snowmobile and hopped out. "The train's stuck!" he called. "There was an avalanche!"

"An avalanche!" Chris cried. "Is anybody hurt?"

"Can't tell," Wally said, going inside. "It blocked the road to Crystal Highlands. It's gonna take some time to dig them out."

They all followed Wally inside. Johnny said, "I'll call the railroad station and see what I can find out."

"First thing we should do," Jesse said, "is get them skiers in here where it's warm."

Johnny stopped and turned to Jesse. Then he smiled. "Why, you old claim jumper, you," he said. "I like the way you think. Sue, get out the steaks, and whip up a batch of cheese fondue! We're going to be overflowing with skiers before the day is out!"

Overflowing turned out to be an understatement. Fortunately, most of the skiers were traveling in groups, and they didn't mind doubling and tripling up in rooms at the Grand Imperial.

Some of the passengers had been a little shaken up when the train had jolted to a stop because of the avalanche. But no one had been hurt. Most of the skiers were actually enjoying the sudden change of plans, behaving as though they'd been granted an unexpected holiday, even if it was in the middle of their vacations.

Johnny was frantically trying to keep up with the guests as they arrived at the registration desk. Wally led the horse-drawn sleigh up to the entrance and let off another load of people.

As they walked into the hotel, one woman in the group said, "This is the most exciting thing that's ever happened to me!"

"Me, too," her friend giggled. "But I still don't know what could have caused the avalanche."

The first woman said, "Probably just some freak of nature."

Jesse looked out the doorway at Wally, the explosives expert, and said, "You can say that again."

"Dad," Chris said, coming up to the desk, "in a hot buttered rum, do you heat the butter or the rum first? Mom wants to know."

"What are you asking me for?" Johnny said.

"It isn't in the bartender's guide."

"Get Mom to come to the desk," he said. "I'll take over the bar."

He saw Wally fall into an easy chair, exhausted.

"Up, up!" Johnny said. "Go back and get another load. They'll have that train dug out pretty soon."

Wally dragged himself from the chair and out the door. Sue went behind the desk, and Johnny took off for the bar.

He didn't know much about mixing drinks, but he knew more than Sue. Besides, he was convinced that most of the guests were in too good a mood to complain if he didn't get the proportions right.

He got himself settled behind the bar and saw his son scoot by. Richard was doubling as busboy and waiter, and loving it.

At the registration desk, the two giggling women had just signed in. Jesse threw a critical look at their luggage — two full-sized suitcases and a small cosmetics bag.

Sue hit the bell on the desk and turned to the next customers. Jesse walked over, picked up the cosmetics bag, and turned in the direction of the stairs.

"What about the other bags?" one of the women asked.

Jesse stopped, turned, and looked at the suitcases. "Better bring them along," he said. "Can't leave them in the lobby."

On the way up the stairs, they passed a man carrying a glass of water. He was obviously on his way to register a complaint.

"Do you work here?" he asked Jesse.

"Would I be carrying this if I didn't?" Jesse said, holding up the cosmetics bag.

The man thrust the glass under Jesse's nose. "There's a *fish* in my drink!" he said angrily.

Jesse looked into the glass. Sure enough, a tiny guppy was swimming around in it.

"Shhh!" Jesse whispered. "Not so loud! If word gets around, everybody'll want one!"

He walked on up the stairs. Dumbfounded, the guest looked from Jesse to the glass, and back to Jesse again. Then he turned and went back toward his room.

It was well after midnight. The fires in the three first-floor fireplaces were burning down. All the lights were out except for the one that burned over the entrance.

Johnny closed the registration book while Sue poked at one of the fires. The rest of the staff were sound asleep, as were most of the guests. The last three holdouts had just left the dining room and were on their way up to their rooms.

Johnny stepped out onto the front porch, leaving the door open behind him. He took several deep breaths, enjoying the cold night air, and watching the smoke rise as he exhaled. He stretched out his arms and shivered.

"Hi," Sue said from behind him.

"Hi," he said, turning. "Come on out for a minute. Tired?"

"Exhausted. You?"

"Yeah, me too," he said. "But *happy* exhausted. Do you know what I mean?"

Sue nodded and put her arm around his waist. They stood looking out at the snow glistening in the moonlight.

"People seem to like the place," Johnny said. "If we can keep them happy for two weeks, we'll have more than enough to pay back the loan."

He leaned over and kissed her cheek. "Then," he said, "we just wait till they spread the word for us. That'll be better than a hundred ads."

She smiled at him. "I'd better put some sheets on the couches for us," she said. "Who did you give our room to?"

"Miss Ogelvie," he said. "The lawyer from Santa Barbara. I just saw her going upstairs a minute ago."

They were interrupted by a shriek from one of the bedrooms.

"Oh, Lord!" Sue said. "What now?"

They hurried inside and bounded up the stairs. A second scream told them the trouble was in their own bedroom.

"It's Miss Ogelvie!" Johnny said over his shoulder. He ran to the door of his room and pounded on it.

"Miss Ogelvie! Miss Ogelvie, what's wrong?"

The door flew open, and they saw Miss Ogelvie in a flannel nightgown. Her face was pale, and she looked ready for a third scream.

"What happened?" Johnny asked, looking

around the room. It was too dark in there for him to see anything.

She pointed into the room, but turned her face to the hall, unable to face whatever the horror was. "I had just turned out the lights," she said, her voice shaking with fear. "I was climbing into bed, when —"

She broke off, sobbing, unable to continue. By now, several guests were in the hall, trying to find out what all the noise was about.

Sue stayed in the hall as Johnny carefully stepped into the bedroom. She watched his tension disappear as soon as he saw what the trouble was.

"All right!" he yelled. "Get out of there!" He stepped further into the room. "You ought to be ashamed of yourself!"

He came out of the room, pulling Strongheart by the scruff of the neck. Some of the guests laughed. Sue smiled. Miss Ogelvie stared stonily at the intruder as he was led out of the room.

"I'm very sorry, Miss Ogelvie," he said. "Until today, this was our bedroom. Strongheart didn't understand. It won't happen again."

"Thank you," she said, without changing her expression. She stepped into her room and closed the door.

The other guests went back to their rooms, and Johnny and Sue led Strongheart downstairs. Strongheart kept turning his head to look back at the closed door of his bedroom.

"Come on, fella," Johnny said. "I'll show you your new sleeping quarters."

"We'd better be extra nice to Miss Ogelvie for a few days," Sue said. "Finding that huge animal in your bed *could* be quite a shock."

"Right," Johnny said. "I was really worried there for a minute. Wouldn't it be terrific if this were the worst problem we had for the next two weeks?"

"Yes, it would be," Sue said. "But don't count on it. "Tomorrow, everybody's going to want to *ski*."

A momentary fear shot through Johnny's body. He pictured his own skiing experience of a few weeks earlier. Then he erased the picture from his mind.

"Sure," he said, trying to sound cheerful. "That's what they're here for, after all."

As they cleaned up the dining room after breakfast, Sue and Johnny looked out the window and saw their ski lodge in full operation. From where they stood, it looked like a dream come true.

At the top of the long slope, Wally stood waiting for his class of beginners to assemble. While they gathered, he was off to the side reading a book. Nobody noticed the title of the book, and that was just as well. Their instructor was reading *Fundamentals of Good Skiing*.

Down near the lower end of the slope, Jesse was ready to haul up his next load of skiers. He and Johnny had discovered an old steam engine in a garage near the back of the hotel. With some help from Wally, and a lot of luck, they had gotten it into working condition for very little money.

A "donkey engine," Jesse had told them it

was called. They used to be useful for lugging heavy logs up hills.

Now the donkey engine was pulling skiers up the hill on a rope-and-pulley arrangement that Jesse and Wally had erected. This was the job that had taken the last remaining dollars of the loan from Ridgeway's bank.

Jesse gave a toot on the engine's whistle and started up the hill. As he chugged along, he sang "Casey Jones," or as much of it as he could remember. He was enjoying his new status as chief engineer.

When Wally's students were ready, he stuck his book into his parka, patted his ski instructor's arm band, and moved to join his class.

A dozen people stood around on skis, waiting to be told what to do. Wally paused for a few seconds, running through his mind the six pages he had just memorized. When he was sure he had it all down, he greeted his students.

"Okay, class," he said, "the lesson today will be straight running—or *schussing*, as it's called."

He smiled at them. They smiled back. Then he quoted from the book. "The first thing the neophyte skier must do is relax. There is really nothing to fear. Now, when you *schuss*, the skis are held close together with the weight distributed equally like this."

Wally demonstrated. Then he looked up and saw 12 faces smiling blankly at him.

"Maybe this isn't the best way to do it," he said. "How about one of you stepping over here and trying it with me?"

As he waited, he looked them over. One middle-aged woman seemed very nervous. Since no one volunteered, he pointed to her and said, "Come on, Miss. I'll show you how."

"Me?" she said. "Well, maybe one of the others would like to — "

"Nothing to be afraid of," Wally said confidently. "Come on. I'll go down with you."

She sidled over and stood next to him. Wally got into position and leaned forward.

"Like this," he said. "Yes, that's it. That's it," Wally said, moving along with her. "You're doing fine."

"Ohhhhhh!" she screamed. They were picking up speed, and she grabbed his hand. She was moving faster and faster, and she gripped his hand tightly. Wally tried to get free, but he couldn't loosen her grip.

"Slow down!" he yelled. "Stop!"

Without intending to, she finally let go of his hand. Her body turned sideways, she slowed, then fell into the snow, her skis in the air.

She stood up to brush snow from her clothes and looked down the slope. There was Wally, speeding in the direction of the steam engine.

Jesse had heard Wally's screams, just as he was about to bring another group of skiers up the hill. He had uncurled a rope that was tied to the back of the engine. This was now lying across the snow, crossing the path that Wally was cutting into the slope.

"Grab the rope!" Jesse yelled, pointing, then waving his arms, then pointing again. "Grab the rope, Wally!"

As Wally neared the rope, Jesse hopped back onto the donkey engine. Speeding down the hill, Wally bent low enough to touch the snow. When he reached the rope, he grabbed it. Jesse started the steam engine up the hill, hoping to stop Wally's progress. As he inched up the hill, he frantically tooted the whistle over and over.

Sue had seen the whole thing from the dining room window. She was on the phone calling for help.

"I don't know what's wrong!" she said. "But the steam whistle is blowing like crazy! Yes, yes, send an ambulance!"

Jesse, moving up the hill, pulled the rope taut, and Wally's forward progress slowed. He quickly tied the rope around his waist, not trusting himself to be able to hold on much longer.

In a desperate effort to move as fast as possible, Jesse had pushed the engine as hard as he could. But the engine was too old to take the extra strain.

As he neared the top of the hill, Jesse heard the steam engine conk out. He was on his way down the hill just as Wally came to a halt.

Wally looked up and saw the steam engine bearing down on him. "Stop it!" he called.

As Jesse passed him, he answered, "You tell me how! I'll be glad to!"

Seeing what was about to happen, Wally tried to get the rope untied from around his waist. He fumbled with the knot, but he couldn't loosen it. The rope was taut again, and he was being pulled in the direction of the hotel.

Sue had just hung up the phone in the dining room. She suddenly realized that the steam whistle had become a lot louder. She ran to the window just in time to see Johnny jump out of the engine's way. It knocked over a pile of logs and came crashing through the dining room wall.

"Jesse!" she screamed. "Where's Wally?"

"He'll be along in a minute," Jesse yelled, as he sped past her and out through the opposite wall.

A bewildered-looking Wally came skiing through a few seconds later. Sue watched him come in through the first wall and go out the second. By now, Johnny had come back inside, and they both ran to the hole in the wall through which the steam engine—and Wally—had departed.

They stood there and looked out. The engine was buried in a snow bank, a total wreck. Jesse was carefully climbing out, and Wally was trying to lift himself from the ground.

Chris came running up to help. She tore his skis off and grabbed him around the chest to lift him.

"Ow!" Wally yelled.

"What's wrong?" she asked, letting go of him.

He got to his feet. "My arm," he said. "I can't lift it."

"Maybe it's broken!" she said. "Dad, call a doctor! Wally's hurt!"

"There's an ambulance on the way," Sue said.

Jesse walked slowly up to the building and through the hole in the wall. He looked it over, then crossed the room to evaluate the other one. He watched Sue, Johnny, and Richard surveying the damage to windows, furniture, and dishes.

"Anybody know where a good bellhop can find a quiet job?" he asked.

◇ ◇ 13 ◇ ◇

The sun was shining into the office through the window behind Mr. Ridgeway's back. That meant it was in Johnny's eyes.

"Then it went through one side of the hotel and came out the other," Johnny said, squinting up at Ridgeway. "It tore up the dining room, and — well, things are a mess."

Ridgeway stared down at him, showing no emotion. "And your guests," he said. "How are they enjoying half a hotel?"

"Well — "

"They're not, are they? As a matter of fact, they've all left, haven't they?"

"Yes," Johnny said weakly. "But they all said they'd had a good time while it lasted."

Miss Wiggington came in and put some papers on Ridgeway's desk. As she turned to leave, she gave Johnny a small smile. She left the door open and sat outside at her own desk.

"What you're saying, Baxter," Ridgeway said, "is that you won't be able to meet your obligation to the bank this month."

"Not if I want to do the necessary repairs," Johnny said. "But I wanted to talk to you about an extension on the loan."

"Baxter," Ridgeway said, standing and walking around to the front of his desk. "Baxter, Baxter, Baxter. I like you, you know."

"Thank you, Mr. Ridgeway," Johnny said, standing to face him. He swallowed hard, then added, "I like you too."

"And because I like you, Baxter, I'm going to do you a favor. I won't let you pour more good money into a rat hole. I won't let you force me to foreclose on your loan. I'm going to take that dump off your hands, Baxter."

Miss Wiggington sat outside, shaking her head. "He wins again," she thought. "And such a nice family, too."

"Baxter," Ridgeway went on, "I'm going to *give* you $200 out of my own pocket. That's enough for you and that sweet little family of yours to get back to New York, where you belong. Now what do you say to that?"

Johnny stared at him for a long time. Miss Wiggington sat outside, waiting for the inevitable surrender. Ridgeway smiled his broadest smile. At last, Johnny spoke.

"That's very kind of you, sir. But I still have till the end of the month."

Ridgeway's eyes widened. How could this young upstart be such an ingrate?

"The end of the month," he intoned, "is only five days away!"

"I know," Johnny said, heading for the door. "But I'll come up with something."

"We'll see, Baxter," Ridgeway called after him. "See you in five days."

Johnny closed the office door behind him. Miss Wiggington gave him a big smile. "Hang in there," she said.

"Thanks," he said, returning the smile. "I will. For five more days, anyway."

Later that day, Johnny and Sue sat in the sleigh. The horse walked slowly through the snow, and they rode in silence.

They could see Chris and Wally at the top of the ski slope, looking off in the opposite direction. Wally's right arm was in a sling. His other arm was around Chris's shoulders.

Inside the hotel, Jesse and Richard sat in their coats in front of a fire. They were playing checkers, and Richard had just ended a game with a triple jump.

"Another game?" Jesse asked.

"No, thanks," Richard said. "I think I'll see if I can dig up some road maps."

"Road maps?" Jesse asked. "What for?"

"To see if I can figure out a different route back to New York," Richard said. "No sense going back the same way we came. Might as well see some different scenery."

"Guess you've got a point there," Jesse said, eyeing the boy sadly. "Might as well get something out of the trip back home."

14

Five days later, both the month and the Grand Imperial Ski Lodge were coming to an end. The station wagon stood outside the main entrance, loaded in the same way it had been for the trip from New York. Sue sat on the porch, dreamily staring at a wheel of one of the bicycles that stood on the roof of the car.

Through the spokes, she could see Chris and Wally walking slowly back to the hotel from the top of the hill. Every few yards they'd stop and say something to each other. Then they'd continue their slow descent.

The silence was broken by Richard's voice. "Hi, Mom," he called as he trudged through the snow up to the entrance.

"Hi," she said, smiling weakly. "I was beginning to worry that you might not be back in time."

"What a dumb town," he said. "Couldn't find a road atlas anywhere." He came up to the porch and sat in a chair next to hers.

"Don't worry about it," she said. "We'll stop in Denver and pick one up."

"Okay," he said, brightening a little. "Where's Dad?"

"In the kitchen. He decided to empty the refrigerator. I think we're going to wind up with a lunch big enough for the Colorado National Guard."

"I'll give him a hand," Richard said, getting up and going inside.

As Richard walked through the dining room, he smiled at Strongheart, who was lazing in front of the dying fire. On the other side of the room, Jesse sat with his chair facing the hole he had made with the steam engine. He had patched it up, but now he seemed to be marveling all over again at what he had accomplished. Richard didn't disturb him and went on into the kitchen.

"Can I give you a hand, Dad?"

"Thanks," Johnny said. "It's all finished, but you can help me carry it out to the car."

He picked up two large bags filled with food. Richard picked up the third bag and followed him out to the car.

Sue helped them put the bags into the back seat. Wally and Chris stepped up on the porch, trying to outdo each other in looking glum.

"Anybody have the time?" Chris asked.

Johnny looked at his watch. "He should be here any minute," he said. At the sound of an approaching car, he added, "Count on Ridgeway to be right on time."

Johnny slowly went inside, and everyone else followed. Although no one mentioned it, it seemed right that Ridgeway should come in to meet them. Meeting him at the door would seem too friendly for what was about to happen.

The car pulled up, Ridgeway driving, and Miss Wiggington sitting in the front seat next to him. Ridgeway bounced out of the car with a handful of legal papers in his hand. When he turned to close the door, he saw his secretary still sitting, staring straight ahead.

"Well?" he said.

"Do I really have to go in with you?" she asked, still staring.

"Yes," he said firmly. "I need you to witness the signatures."

She took a deep breath, let out a sigh, and opened her door. She got out and slammed it hard.

"I'd rather not have any part of this," she said.

"Business is business, Miss Wiggington."

"*This* kind of business," she said, "is pleasure for you." She was surprised at her own courage in saying this to him. But he seemed to take it as a compliment.

Already up on the porch, he said cheerfully, "You know, you're right. There is nothing more satisfying than a well-planned deal."

She stared angrily at his back as he rapped on the front door. "It's open," Johnny called from inside.

The family — including Wally and Jesse — was in a close semicircle around the small fire. Strongheart growled as Ridgeway stepped into the lobby, followed by Miss Wiggington.

Richard sat on the floor next to Strongheart and patted his head to calm him. Everyone else stood staring either at Ridgeway or at the papers in his hand.

"Good afternoon, everyone!" Ridgeway said with a smile that no one returned.

Miss Wiggington caught Sue's eye and gave her a sympathetic look. Sue responded with a small smile.

"Well, Baxter," Ridgeway intoned, "we might as well get this over with. I don't like it any more than you do."

Miss Wiggington shot him a nasty look. He

was really going to make this as hard for her as possible.

Ridgeway walked over to the bar and put the papers on it. He took a pen from his pocket and laid it next to the papers.

"This is a quit-claim deed, Baxter," he said. "You just sign everywhere you see an X, and we'll be all finished."

Johnny walked to the bar and picked up the pen. He looked at the papers and hesitated.

"Now, don't feel that way about it," Ridgeway said. "There are lots of businesses you could do well in. For instance, have you thought about insurance?"

"Quite a bit," Johnny said with a rueful smile.

"Well, there you are then," Ridgeway said.

Miss Wiggington looked from Johnny to Sue. This ceremony was getting more painful by the second. She looked down at Richard, who was now snuggled up next to Strongheart. Next to them, she saw Wally holding Chris's hand, as Chris tried to keep from crying. And there sat old Jesse, showing more hatred than Miss Wiggington would have imagined him capable of.

"Think of it this way, Baxter," her boss proclaimed. "You're not losing a ski lodge. You're providing a home for wayward boys."

At his solemn tone, something snapped inside Miss Wiggington. Let him be a snake if he wanted to. She didn't have to crawl along with him!

"Wayward boys, my foot!" she said through clenched teeth.

"Miss Wiggington!" Ridgeway said, turning to her. "Be careful what you say!"

"Why should I?" she said. "Fire me if you want! I can go to Denver and make twice as much as what you pay me! And I won't have to wallow in slime for it!"

Ridgeway had never heard anything like it in his life, least of all from one of his employees. He was genuinely hurt.

"Slime?" he said weakly. "That may be overstating—"

Ignoring him, she turned to Johnny. "Forget the home for wayward boys," she said. "You know why he wants this place? Because 3,000 acres of Douglas fir goes with it!"

Everyone stared at Miss Wiggington. Then, as though they were watching a tennis match, all eyes moved to Ridgeway.

"Really?" was all Johnny could come up with.

"Darn right!" Miss Wiggington said, warming up to her new role as truth-dispenser. "Jacob Barnsworth granted the land to the Ute Indians in these hills. It was to be theirs as long as they occupied it."

Jesse, excited beyond control, jumped between Johnny and Miss Wiggington. "She's telling it right, Johnny!" he said. "They didn't have to do nothing for it. Not like when he gave 200 acres for the town of Silver Hill. That was on condition that they build a church, a library, and two hospitals." He turned to Miss Wiggington to explain, "One for folks and one for animals."

"Dad!" Richard said. Something he had just heard startled him.

"Just a minute, Richard," Johnny said.

"In any case, Mr. Baxter," Miss Wiggington said, "the Utes have all left or died off. So the timberland automatically goes back to the Barnsworth estate. That's *you*, Mr. Baxter. And now you know what you're actually signing away."

"Dad, listen!" Richard said.

"Not now, Richard," Johnny said. He turned to Ridgeway. "Is that why you want this place?" he asked. "Douglas firs?"

"You're gonna cut down those woods in back

of town?" Wally said angrily.

Ridgeway ignored him and spoke only to Johnny. "Let's stick to facts, Baxter. At this point, it doesn't matter *why* I want this property. All that matters now is that you can't meet the payment, and it's due today! If you don't sign these papers, I'll be forced to start foreclosure proceedings in the morning!"

"Dad!" Richard said, pulling on Johnny's arm.

"Richard!" Johnny said, pulling his arm away. "This is very important! Now, I told you—"

The hurt look on his son's face made him stop in midsentence. The angry look faded from his face, as he thought of how hard all this was for everyone.

"I'm sorry, Richard," he said softly. "I shouldn't have yelled at you. What was it you wanted to say?"

Richard relaxed visibly, glad to have finally got his father's attention. Instead of addressing his father, though, he turned to Jesse.

"What did you say a minute ago?" Richard asked. "About what the town had to do to keep the 200 acres?"

Jesse looked confused. "They had to build a church," he said. "And two hospitals." Suddenly, his face began to break into a wide grin. "And a library!" he shouted.

"Right!" Richard shouted over his voice. "I was just in town looking for road maps! And one thing I found out is that the nearest library is in Evergreen, 50 miles from Silver Hill!"

"That means," Sue said slowly, "the town hasn't lived up to Jacob Barnsworth's conditions."

"And that means—" Johnny said, turning to face Ridgeway. The banker was slowly edging toward the door.

"That means," Johnny repeated, "the 200 acres also belong to the estate!"

"That's ridiculous!" Ridgeway said, without much conviction.

"Not ridiculous at all!" Miss Wiggington said, smiling. "If the restrictions were violated, the property goes back to Barnsworth! Or his heirs!"

Ridgeway had now opened the door. He paused long enough to hear his former secretary add her final touch.

"Mr. Baxter," she said, "you just may own the whole town of Silver Hill. Including his bank!" She gleefully pointed at Ridgeway, who stepped back into the room.

"Now, Johnny," he said.

"Make it Mr. Baxter," Johnny said.

"Yes," Ridgeway said. "Mr. Baxter. I see no reason why we can't work this out. Why, a ski lodge might be the best thing that's ever happened to Silver Hill. Uh—I wonder if I could have a glass of water—and a couple of aspirins."

"Sure, Mr. Ridgeway," Chris said laughing. "You'll find them in the pantry next to the stove."

With his head throbbing, Ridgeway walked into the kitchen. His headache wasn't helped by what he heard. He was rocked by a loud cheer from seven happy people, and a considerable amount of barking from a very large St. Bernard.

By twilight, the celebration was beginning to wind itself down. It was almost time for dinner. If you stood near the side of one of the smaller slopes, you would have seen a short parade go by as everyone headed back toward the lodge.

First in the parade was Richard, who zipped by with the confidence of a new skier with a natural talent. He was followed by Chris, and then Wally, who'd taught both of them everything they knew.

Shortly after them came two skiers less

sure of themselves, but having just as much fun. Sue and Johnny used their poles, keeping to a slower pace, and laughed out loud all the way down the slope.

Two large inner tubes followed them, one carrying Jesse, the other carrying Miss Wiggington, who sang at the top of her voice.

Bearing down on them was the cover of a garbage can that propelled Strongheart in the direction of dinner. As he passed Miss Wigginton and Jesse, he gave a woof that was loud enough to echo throughout the dimly-lit valley. He was on his way to dinner at the Grand Imperial Ski Lodge.